Joey!

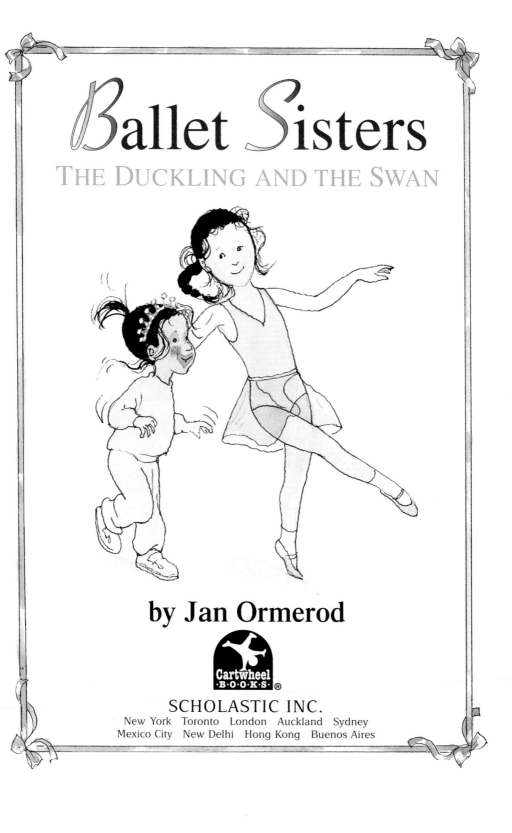

Ballet Sisters
THE DUCKLING AND THE SWAN

by Jan Ormerod

Cartwheel
·B·O·O·K·S·®

SCHOLASTIC INC.

New York   Toronto   London   Auckland   Sydney
Mexico City   New Delhi   Hong Kong   Buenos Aires

Copyright © 2007 by Jan Ormerod.
All rights reserved. Published by Scholastic Inc.
SCHOLASTIC, CARTWHEEL BOOKS, and associated logos are trademarks and/or registered trademarks of Scholastic Inc.

Library of Congress Cataloging-in-Publication Data.

Ormerod, Jan.
Ballet sisters : the duckling and the swan / by Jan Ormerod.
p. cm. -- "Cartwheel books."
Summary: Sylvie and her older sister dance their way through make-believe adventures that include princesses, fairy queens, swans, and ducklings.
ISBN 0-439-82281-5 (hardcover: alk. paper)
[1. Sisters--Fiction. 2. Imagination--Fiction. 3. Ballet--Fiction. 4. Dancers--Fiction.] I. Title.
PZ7.O634Bal 2007
[E]--dc22   2006002575

ISBN-13: 978-0-439-82281-7
ISBN-10: 0-439-82281-5
10 9 8 7 6 5 4 3 2 1   7 8 9 10 11/0
Printed in Singapore
First printing, February 2007

For Grace

DUCKY DANCER

Mom and Sylvie

get me from school.

"I am a swan," I say.

"And you are a duckling."

"I'm a ducky," Sylvie says.

At home, Sylvie
and I dress up.
Then we dance.

"I'm a princess," I say.

"You must bow to me."

"Okay," Sylvie says.

We dance into the garden.

"I'm a fairy queen," I say.

"And you are an elf."

Sylvie cries, "I don't want
to be an elf."

Mom sweeps Sylvie up
and carries her
from flower to flower.

"Sylvie is a buzzing bee,"
says Mom.

Then I am a swan again.

And Sylvie is a duckling.

She waddles.

She flaps her wings.

She takes a bow.

BRAIDS

On Saturday, I get ready
for ballet class.
I wash my face and hands.

Sylvie washes her face
and hands, too.

I clean my teeth.

Sylvie cleans her teeth, too.

I put on my leotard and tights.

Sylvie puts on her socks.

I put on sweatpants
and sneakers.
So does Sylvie.

I put my slippers, sweater, snack,
and drink into my ballet bag.
Sylvie puts a truck, a toy mouse, a
snack, and a drink into her backpack.

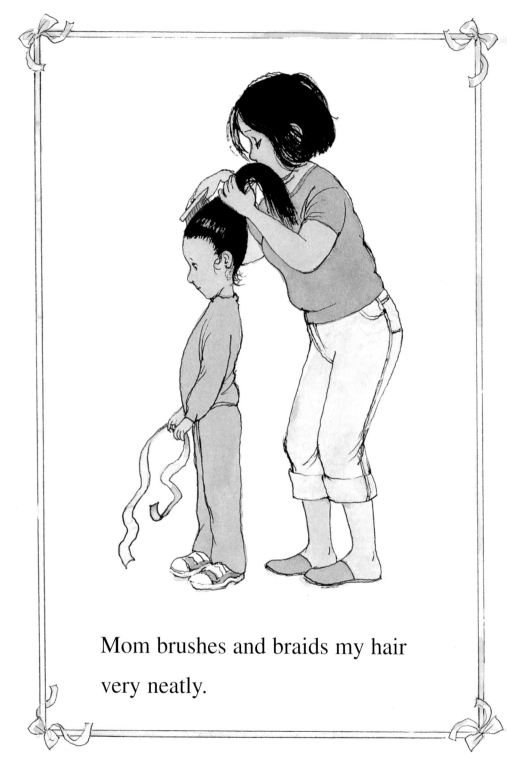

Mom brushes and braids my hair
very neatly.

Sylvie tries to make her hair neat.

She cuts a piece that sticks out.

It is lopsided,
so she cuts some more.

Now it is very lopsided.

Sylvie cries.

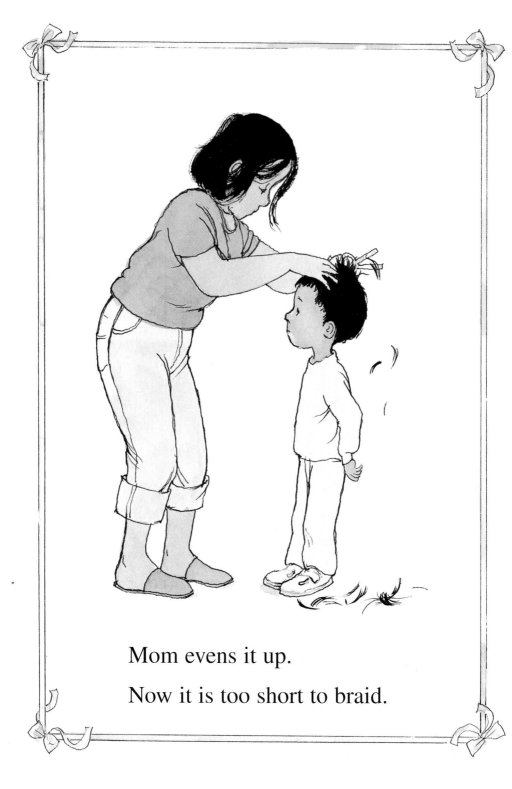

Mom evens it up.

Now it is too short to braid.

Sylvie cries again.

I have an idea. I take old tights
from the dress-up box.

I cut each leg into three strips and
make braids for Sylvie to wear.
Sylvie is happy again.

MISS TRISHA'S CLASS

Hand in hand, we skip
to the church hall.

I go into Miss Trisha's ballet class.

Sylvie waits outside for me.

In class, I spin and jump
and pose to the music.

Sylvie can hear it, too.

She quacks, waddles, and flaps.

On the way home, I say,

"I am a swan."

"And I am a duckling,"

says Sylvie.